—

COULD YOU BE

A BIG MOUNTAIN

SKIER?

BY BLAKE HOENA

CAPSTONE PRESS
a capstone imprint

You Choose Books is published by Capstone Press, an imprint
of Capstone.
1710 Roe Crest Drive
North Mankato, Minnesota 56003
www.capstonepub.com

Library of Congress Cataloging-in-Publication Data is available on the Library of
Congress website.
ISBN: 978-1-4966-8149-2 (library binding)
ISBN: 978-1-4966-8691-6 (paperback)
ISBN: 978-1-4966-8162-1 (ebook PDF)

Summary: Do you have what it takes to freeski down a steep slope? Test your skills
against the extreme and dangerous sport of big mountain skiing.

Image Credits
Alamy: Cavan Images, 42–43, 70, Chris Hellier, 100, Folio Images, 59, Randy
Lincks, 17, 109, robertharding, 21, StockShot, 66–67; Getty Images: Cameron
Spencer, 92–93, Spinkle, 35; iStockphoto: stockstudioX, 4–5, Tainar, 6; Newscom:
Carl R. Battreall, 96, picture-alliance/blickwinkel/P. Royer, 85, ZUMA Press/
James Healey, 23; Shutterstock: mjaud, 27, Olga Lyubochkina, 79, OutdoorWorks,
77, Pascal Rateau, 75, Pierre Leclerc, 12, Roberto Caucino, 55, sirtravelalot, cover, 1,
Stereo Lights, 48, tale, 53

Editorial Credits
Editor: Michelle Parkin; Designer: Brann Garvey; Media Researcher: Eric Gohl;
Production Specialist: Tori Abraham

Printed in the United States of America
3342

TABLE OF CONTENTS

ABOUT YOUR ADVENTURE 5

CHAPTER 1
WINTER VACATION..7

CHAPTER 2
HITTING THE TERRAIN PARK.................................13

CHAPTER 3
UP IN THE ALPS...49

CHAPTER 4
HELI-SKIING 71

CHAPTER 5
SKIING THROUGH HISTORY 101

BRIEF BIOGRAPHIES 106
OTHER PATHS TO EXPLORE..........................108
GLOSSARY 110
READ MORE 111
INTERNET SITES 111
INDEX 112

ABOUT YOUR ADVENTURE

Can you be a big mountain skier?
There's only one way to find out. Down!

Chapter One sets the scene. Then you choose which path to read. Follow the directions at the bottom of the page as you read the stories. The decisions you make will change your outcome. After you finish one path, go back and read the others for new perspectives and more adventures.

CHAPTER 1

WINTER VACATION

Outside, the world is a winter wonderland. Big, fluffy flakes fall from the sky and cover everything in a blanket of snow.

You sit with your friends in the school cafeteria. The world around you is abuzz. It's a week before winter break. Everyone is more interested in talking about their plans for the holidays than they are in eating lunch.

"That's some great powder out there," your friend Tess says, looking out the window. "Are you thinking of hitting the slopes with us over break?"

"Maybe," you reply. "I don't know if I'll have time."

"Why, are you going somewhere?" your friend Tou asks.

"I think so," you say with smile. "My dad's been hinting at going on a ski trip."

You know your friends are jealous. They're both amazing skiers. Tess is also an expert snowboarder. Every chance you get, the three of you hit the slopes at the ski hill near your house. It is a fun place to hang out and get in some runs. But you've been dying to try somewhere more challenging, something a little more like your favorite influencer, Steezy. The guy is a skiing superstar! He shows his followers what it's like to ski some of the most extreme places in the world. Your dad has been promising all year long to take you on a ski trip. You hope it's someplace Steezy has been.

"Do you know where you're going?" Tess asks you.

You shake your head. "No idea."

"Do you think you'll get to take a friend?" Tou asks with a wink.

You shrug. "I can ask."

The rest of the day drags on. You can't stop checking the time. The seconds tick away far too slowly. Finally, the last bell rings. You say goodbye to your friends and wait for your bus. All the snow has made it late. It's a long, slow ride home as you watch the snow pile up. But you don't mind. Extra snow means better skiing. You'd love to be hitting the slopes with your friends.

When you get to your house, you find your dad in the dining room.

"Hey, Dad," you say. "Whatcha doing?"

Spread out across the dining room table are various maps. You see British Columbia, Italy, and Alaska.

"Trying to plan our trip," he says. "Take a look," he says pointing to the maps. "I've got it nailed down to three places."

The first is British Columbia. Vancouver, British Columbia, hosted the Winter Olympics back in 2010. Events ranging from cross-country skiing and bobsledding to ski jumping were held at Whistler Olympic Park, north of Vancouver. The Whistler area has some of the best terrain parks in the world. It would be a great place to get in some freeskiing, a type of skiing that can involve doing jumps and tricks.

Then there is Monterosa Ski in northern Italy. This resort sits at the foot of Monte Rosa, the second tallest mountain in the Alps. The Alps stretch across south central Europe, from eastern France to Austria. It is where the sport of alpine skiing was born. Monterosa Ski is a famous destination for backcountry skiing.

Lastly, there's Alaska. The largest state in the country is mostly wilderness, with the Alaska Mountain range in the southeast and the Brooks Range stretching across the north. Aircraft are needed to reach the most remote areas. Heli-skiing is popular up there. This is probably one of the most extreme types of skiing. You get dropped off by helicopter on a mountain. Then it's just you and your skis with lots of untouched snow. This is often called free-ride skiing because there are no groomed trails or established runs. You make your own path downhill.

"So, where would you like to go?" your dad asks.

All three sound fantastic, but you can only pick one. Where are you going?

TO TRAVEL TO BRITISH COLUMBIA FOR SOME FREESKIING, TURN TO PAGE 13.
TO BACKCOUNTRY SKI IN MONTEROSA SKI, TURN TO PAGE 49.
TO HELI-SKI IN ALASKA, TURN TO PAGE 71.

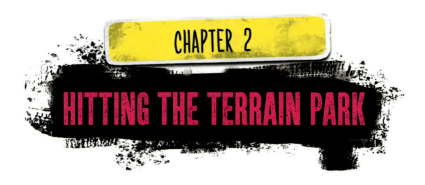

CHAPTER 2

HITTING THE TERRAIN PARK

The town of Whistler is located about an hour and a half north of Vancouver. It is tucked within the Fitzsimmons Range in the southwestern part of the province. The ski resort there is called Whistler Blackcomb, because it includes both Whistler Mountain and Blackcomb Peak. There is even a gondola that carries tourists the 2 miles between the peaks.

But what interests you most about Whistler Blackcomb is its terrain parks. There are five parks total, with hundreds of jumps, rails, and other obstacles for tricks. There's even a huge halfpipe.

TURN THE PAGE.

"Can we go to Whistler?" you ask your dad. "It'd be so cool to hit the terrain parks there."

"Sound great," your dad says. "Why don't you invite one of your friends along?"

"Really?" you ask.

"Yeah," your dad replies. "I won't be able to keep up with you on the terrain park. It'd be good if you buddied up with someone."

You immediately think of Tess. She'd love to hit the terrain parks at Whistler Blackcomb. If you invite her, you could work on some snowboarding tricks. But then again, Tou asked to come along. He's more of a skier. And on his trick skis, he can do anything that Tess can do on her snowboard. The real question is, do you want to go snowboarding or skiing at Whistler?

TO SKI WITH TOU, TURN TO PAGE 15.
TO SNOWBOARD WITH TESS, TURN TO PAGE 19.

You have been wanting to go on a ski trip all along. Tou is one of the best skiers you know. So, you give him a call.

"What's up?" Tou answers.

"Hey, guess where my dad's taking me," you say, but before giving him a chance to answer, you add, "Whistler Blackcomb!"

"You'll be hitting some top-notch slopes," Tou exclaims. "I'm jealous."

"You don't have to be," you say. "You could come with us. My dad said to invite a friend."

"Whoa, no way!" he shouts.

TURN THE PAGE.

Over the next few days, you and Tou get your gear together while your dad makes travel arrangements.

Before you know it, winter break begins and you're driving up to Whistler. You are excited to see the snow-capped peaks rise up all around you. But after a long day of travel, all you have the energy to do is unload your gear from your dad's SUV.

The next morning, you are up bright and early and ready to go.

"Should we hit Whistler Peak first?" your dad asks.

"Yeah," you say.

"Sounds good to me," Tou adds.

You get all your gear ready. You grab your helmet, goggles, and ski boots.

GO TO PAGE 18.

"I'm thinking of bringing my trick skis," Tou says. "What about you?"

Tou's skis are shorter than the skis you normally use. Your longer skis are great for bombing downhill. But shorter skis like Tou's are better for taking sharp turns.

TO USE YOUR LONGER SKIS, TURN TO PAGE 29.
TO USE SHORTER SKIS, TURN TO PAGE 31.

While you were thinking this would be a ski trip, you love to snowboard. It would be amazing to try some of the tricks you've seen pro snowboarders do online.

You give Tess a call.

"Hey, Tess, you won't believe where my dad's taking me," you say. "Whistler Blackcomb!"

"No way!" she exclaims. "I've only dreamed of going there."

"Well . . . you can stop dreaming," you say. "He said I could invite a friend. Are you in?"

"Yeah!" she says.

After your dad has made all the arrangements, the three of you head out.

TURN THE PAGE.

You arrive in Whistler on a bright, sunny day. But it's been a long day of travel. And you still have to unload all of your gear from your dad's SUV. Everyone is ready to relax for the night.

The next morning, your dad asks, "So where do you two want to start?

"The halfpipe!" Tess says excitedly.

There are no halfpipes at the ski hill by your house, so it's something you've been wanting to try.

"Let's hit it," you say.

You get your gear ready, from your goggles to your helmet. Then you and Tess head over to Blackcomb with your snowboards. You get on the New Blackcomb Gondola. It takes you about two-thirds of the way up the mountain.

The halfpipe is just below the terrain parks. As you head there, you see other snowboarders and skiers flying over jumps and grinding across rails.

You head for the Superpipe, the Blackcomb halfpipe. The entry ramp slopes steeply down into a U shape with 18-foot walls.

"Are you ready for this?" Tess asks.

You feel a mix of nervousness and excitement. Even though you've never been here before, the thought of dropping into the halfpipe is exhilarating.

Tess goes first. She drops in and speeds away. You follow a moment later. Snowboarding on the halfpipe is all about doing tricks. But what should you try? You could stick with a trick you know. Or this could be the time to bust out something new and impress the other snowboarders here.

TO TRY A NEW TRICK, TURN TO PAGE 24.
TO DO A TRICK YOU KNOW, TURN TO PAGE 26.

You have done full spins, or 360s, off of jumps back home. But you've wanted to try a frontside 540 for the longest time. This means you would have to spin one and a half times. This is your first run of the day. Why not give it a try?

You drop in the halfpipe. The top is the steepest part, so you can quickly build up speed. Then you lean into your heels. You turn and shoot up the side of the halfpipe. As you fly up, you twist your body hard. You begin to spin around as you launch into the air.

You make one full spin before you start to drop back down. But you are going faster than you are comfortable with, and you rotate too much.

Suddenly, you hit the wall of the halfpipe with the edge of your snowboard. Your feet are taken right out from under you. You land hard and smack your head on the snow. Then you slide down the rest of the way.

When you stop, Tess is standing over you.

"Take my hand," she says.

When Tess pulls you up, you feel a little wobbly.

"You okay?" Tess asks.

"I dunno," you say. "I hit my head pretty hard."

"You'd better sit down," Tess tells you. "You could have a concussion." She leaves to get you some help.

As your head pounds, you realize you should have waited to try a new trick. Maybe if you were farther down the halfpipe where it wasn't so steep, you could have nailed it. But you won't have a chance to try the trick again today. You likely have a concussion. You'll be stuck inside for a few days.

THE END

TO FOLLOW ANOTHER PATH, TURN TO PAGE 11.

You've wanted to try a one and a half turn for the longest time. But you are at the top of the halfpipe, its steepest section. You'd better wait to try a new trick. At least until you're farther down the halfpipe and you aren't going as fast.

Instead, you decide to do an air-to-fakie. It's a trick you've done many times before. First, you lean on the toe side of your snowboard. Then, you shoot up the wall of the halfpipe. You pop over the coping of the wall with your left foot in front of you. Then, you come straight down so your right foot is in front.

You are surprised by how much air you get! You're glad you went for an easier trick first to get a feel for things.

GO TO PAGE 28.

With your first trick on the halfpipe behind you, it's time to push things a little more. As you zoom down one wall of the halfpipe, you head toward the opposite wall. You perform a trick called a butter, spinning your board in a 180-degree turn. Then you head up the side of the halfpipe.

Next, you want to try a frontside 360 with a toe grab. To do this trick, you sail up over the coping into the air, twisting your body counterclockwise. As you spin, you reach out with your left hand and grab the front end of your snowboard.

You are about three quarters of the way around when you are about to land. Should you keep holding onto your snowboard or let go? It would be impressive to hold on until the last possible moment. But it is showing off a bit. If you let go, you could get your board under you quicker.

TO LET GO OF YOUR SNOWBOARD, TURN TO PAGE 37.
TO HOLD ON, TURN TO PAGE 38.

You grab your long skis. You're skiing on a mountain you've never been on before. You want to stick with the skis with which you are most comfortable.

You and Tou head over to Whistler Mountain. You take the Whistler Village Gondola. It drops you off about three quarters of the way up the mountain.

"Lead the way," Tou says.

You start off. On your longer skis, you are much faster than Tou. When you see the first jump, you head right for it. But you start to struggle as soon as you get in the air. The wind catches your skis and it's hard to control them. You barely hit the landing.

Each time you try to make a sharp turn and set yourself up for a trick, your skis catch on the snow. Your regular skis just aren't right for the terrain park.

TURN THE PAGE.

You have a miserable time tumbling through the snow.

At the end of the day, you're battered and bruised. But Tou is all smiles. He hit trick after trick and you ended up caked in snow.

THE END

TO FOLLOW ANOTHER PATH, TURN TO PAGE 11.

You take Tou's advice and grab shorter skis. You'll be grinding across rails and flying over jumps. The shorter skis will be easier to control.

"Good choice!" Tou says.

The shorter skis are twin-tipped. This means that both the front and back of the skis arc up. This helps you maneuver more easily. And you can ski backward.

Once you're set with your gear, you and Tou head over to Whistler Mountain. Soon, you're on your way up the Whistler Village Gondola. It takes you near the top of the mountain. Then you head over to the terrain park.

When you see the first jump, you head toward it. You're excited to try out your first trick. A 360-degree spin would be a great start.

TURN THE PAGE.

You shoot straight up the jump. Then you bend your knees and prepare to twist your body. For a trick like this, keeping your skis in the right position is just as important as spinning around. Should you look down to see where your skis are positioned or keep looking forward?

TO LOOK DOWN, GO TO PAGE 33.
TO LOOK FORWARD, TURN TO PAGE 34.

You need to be in the correct position, so you look down. You check to make sure your skis are twisted around and facing downhill to land the jump.

But when you look, you lean forward and are thrown off balance. You land with your skis off to the side instead of under you. You can't recover. You reach out with your hand to stop your fall. But when you crash into the snow, you feel a sharp stab of pain shoot up your wrist.

"Ow!" you scream.

Your dad takes you to the hospital. Your wrist is fractured. Your trip might not be over but you're done skiing. You won't be able to hit the slopes again for a few weeks. You spend the rest of the ski trip drinking hot cocoa and watching everyone else do tricks on the halfpipe.

THE END

TO FOLLOW ANOTHER PATH, TURN TO PAGE 11.

Keeping yourself upright and perpendicular to the ground is key when doing a spin like this. Looking down may throw you off balance, and you could crash.

Just before you get in the air, you start to twist your body counterclockwise. You keep your head up and eyes looking ahead as you spin. As you are about to land, you lean forward to match the slope of the hill. *POOF!* You hear your skis hitting the snow. You did it!

Behind you, you hear Tou shout, "Nice one!"

You pump your fist in the air. You're ready to keep going. You head to the next obstacle—a rail. A small ramp leads up to it. You go up the ramp and do a quarter spin to land on the rail. You slide sideways across it.

GO TO PAGE 36.

But that's only half the trick. Once you get near the end of the rail, you need to jump off. It's a chance to do another trick. You could try a half spin, or 180. Or you could really go for it and try a three-quarter spin.

TO DO A 180, TURN TO PAGE 40.
TO DO A THREE-QUARTER SPIN, TURN TO PAGE 41.

You let go so you can bring the toe of your board down as you land. You feel your board hit and slide across the snow as you shoot down the wall.

You've successfully done two tricks and are getting toward the end of the halfpipe. It's not as steep here, so you are going a little slower. You can do one last trick before the end of the halfpipe. This would be the perfect time to try something new, like that frontside 540 you've been wanting to try.

You decide to go for it and head up the side of the halfpipe. You know you're going to need to twist your body hard counterclockwise to do the trick. Do you start twisting just before you get air or just after? If you twist too soon, your board could get caught on the snow. But you are trying to spin around one and a half times. If you start too late, you won't be able to make it all the way around.

TO START TWISTING JUST BEFORE YOU GET AIR, TURN TO PAGE 44.
TO START TWISTING JUST AFTER YOU GET AIR, TURN TO PAGE 46.

Grabbing onto your board is a cool, flashy move. You keep holding on to the toe of your board as you land. But this causes the heel to hit first. The front rips out of your hands and slaps down hard on the snow. The sudden motion throws you off your board and you fall face forward. Stars explode across your vision. And then everything goes black.

Sometime later, you come to. You are lying on a stretcher with Tess kneeling by your side.

"What do you call that?" she asks, trying to smile. "A 360 belly flop?"

"Uh, no . . . what happened?" you ask.

"You were knocked out cold," she says, "I had to go get help."

Maybe if you had let go of your board earlier instead of trying to show off, you would have hit that trick. You would probably be getting ready for another run down the halfpipe. But now, you are on your way to the hospital. Your day on the halfpipe is over.

THE END

TO FOLLOW ANOTHER PATH, TURN TO PAGE 11.

You decide to do a 180-degree spin. As you near the end of the rail, you get ready. You crouch down and bend your knees slightly to jump off. Then you spin your body counterclockwise. You straighten your knees and jump up, lifting your skis off the metal.

You're sliding across the rail sideways, with your left foot in front. You land with the opposite foot in front and slide downhill.

Suddenly, the outer edge of your ski catches on the snow. It knocks your feet out from under you. You crash in a cloud of snow.

If only you had spun around a little farther, you could have nailed the trick. You'll have to remember that on your next run.

THE END

TO FOLLOW ANOTHER PATH, TURN TO PAGE 11.

You are sliding down the rail sideways. If you do a half turn, that means you'll land sideways too. That's not a good idea. It's bound to lead to a crash. So you decide to try a 270.

As you approach the end of rail, you crouch down slightly and twist your body clockwise. Then at the end, you straighten your knees and start to spin counterclockwise. You jump off the rail, lifting your skis off the metal. You spin three quarters of the way around in the air.

You land backward, with the backs of your skis pointing downhill. But with your trick skis, that's not a problem. Soon you're facing forward again.

You wait for Tou to slide up next to you.

"You rocked that!" he exclaims.

TURN THE PAGE.

After nailing your first two tricks on the terrain park, you're feeling pretty pumped.

"Just wait," you say. "We haven't tried the halfpipe over on Blackcomb yet."

Your ski trip has started off in spectacular style. You have nailed your first run down the slopes at Whistler.

THE END

TO FOLLOW ANOTHER PATH, TURN TO PAGE 11.

You know your timing needs to be perfect to do this trick. If you start twisting your body too late, you will end up flailing through the air.

You start to twist just before your right foot shoots above the coping. The back of your board is still on the snow. It provides just enough friction to whip your body around.

Once you're in the air, the board spins with you. You get around one full spin. As you stop to come down, you swing your board around so that your left foot is in front of you.

You shoot down to the bottom of the halfpipe and slide to a stop next to Tess. She greets you with a high five.

"You did a frontside 540!" she yells. "That was amazing."

You have a huge smile on your face. You did three tricks on your way down the halfpipe. You're feeling good and ready to do it again!

THE END

TO FOLLOW ANOTHER PATH, TURN TO PAGE 11.

When you're doing a spin, you need to start twisting at just the right moment. If you twist too soon, your board will cut into the snow. You'll wipe out for sure.

So you wait until you are fully in the air before you twist your body around. But with nothing to push off of, it's nearly impossible to spin in the air. Instead of twisting around, you just end up flailing through the air.

When you come down, you land on your shoulder in the hard-packed snow. Something pops, and you feel instant pain. You end up sliding down the rest of the halfpipe.

Tess walks up to you, spreads her arms are wide, and teases, "Safe!"

But her look quickly changes to one of concern when she sees that you are in pain.

"Are you okay?" she asks, helping you sit up.

"No!" you gasp in pain, grabbing your shoulder.

Tess takes you to get checked out. You find out that you have dislocated your shoulder. It is tender and sore, and you are not allowed to move your arm around. But that's not the worst part. The doctor tells you it will be several weeks before you can get back on the slopes. Your epic ski trip is over before it really got started.

THE END

TO FOLLOW ANOTHER PATH, TURN TO PAGE 11.

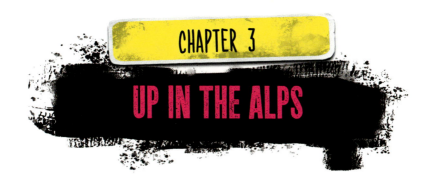

CHAPTER 3

UP IN THE ALPS

Not only is Monterosa Ski a world-famous ski resort, the slopes are perfect for backcountry skiing.

"Monterosa. Definitely," you say.

"I haven't been there in ages," your dad says. "Let's do it!"

That night after your chores, you jump online to video chat with your friends.

"Guess where I'm going?" you ask.

"Uh, the kitchen?" Tou asks with a laugh.

"No, Italy!" you reply. "My dad and I are going to Monterosa Ski!"

TURN THE PAGE.

"You're so lucky," Tess adds. "So, are you going to be able to come skiing with us before your trip?"

You know you're going to be super busy getting ready for Monterosa. You have to make sure all your gear is in tip-top shape. Making sure you have the proper clothing is also important. But it's hard to pass up a chance to ski with your friends.

TO GO SKIING WITH YOUR FRIENDS, TURN TO PAGE 51.
TO SAY NO, TURN TO PAGE 52.

"I'd love to ski with you guys," you say. "And I could use the practice before heading out."

When you ask your dad, he replies, "Good idea. Skiing on this fresh snow should help prepare you for some free-ride skiing at Monterosa."

That weekend, you have a blast with your friends on the slopes. You get in some runs on new snow. But the ski hill in town is nothing compared to where you are going.

Soon, it is time to leave. Your adventure starts with an overseas flight to Italy. From the airport, you take a shuttle bus to the ski resort.

You are exhausted from the long day of travel. You go to bed early. The next morning, you and your dad are raring to go.

"Do you know where you want to go first?" he asks.

TURN TO PAGE 58.

With all the planning you have to do, you don't think you'll have time to join your friends.

"Sorry, I can't," you say. "But when I get back, I'll tell you all about my trip."

The next days are a blur. You gather up all your equipment, from goggles to ski boots. You grab spare gloves and a couple of balaclavas. You decide to leave your skis behind and rent a pair when you get there.

Your trip starts with a long flight over the Atlantic Ocean to Italy. Then you take a shuttle bus to Monterosa Ski. It takes you most of a day to get to your final destination.

"So where should we start?" your dad asks. "Do you want to take it slow and hit the slopes first or go straight to backcountry skiing?"

TO HIT THE SLOPES FIRST, TURN TO PAGE 54.
TO BACKCOUNTRY SKI RIGHT AWAY, TURN TO PAGE 56.

"Let's get in some practice runs on the slopes before the crazy stuff," you tell your dad.

He laughs and nods, "Good idea."

Mont Blanc dwarfs the ski hill back home. Some of the longer runs can take you more than an hour to ski down! That's a lot longer than you are used to.

You are thankful for an easy day checking out the mountain. It builds your confidence for the next part of your adventure.

That night as you are hanging out with your dad, you make a suggestion of where you should ski next.

TURN TO PAGE 58.

You came here to do some extreme skiing, and that's what you want to do.

"Let's skip the slopes," you tell your dad. "We came here to free-ride ski."

"Okay then," he replies. "We'll hit the backcountry tomorrow."

The next morning, you find yourself thousands of feet up in the mountains. In front of you, snow spreads out to the horizon. It is a scary sight. You knew there would be no paths to follow. But you didn't realize you'd be quite this high up. And there is no one to help you if you get into trouble, other than your dad.

Backcountry skiing is much more difficult than you'd thought. The untouched snow drags on your skis and is difficult to turn in. The slopes are much steeper than you are used to. You tumble before you get too far, only to fall again a little farther downhill.

At one point, there is a rock jutting out of the snow in front of you. You are skiing fast. As you try to swerve around it, your skis catch on the snow. Your shoulder slams into the rock, and you are knocked into the snow.

When you try to get up, you can't. You can't put any pressure on your shoulder without feeling pain.

"You may have busted your collarbone," your dad says after helping you up.

Your injury makes for a long trip down. You are unable to ski and trudging through the snow takes forever. You are exhausted and cold by time you get down the mountain. What's worse, because of your injury, you won't be able to do any skiing for the rest of the trip.

THE END

TO FOLLOW ANOTHER PATH, TURN TO PAGE 11.

"Let's try Alagna," you say.

You've done your research on Monterosa Ski. Alagna Valsesia is a town at the southeastern foot of the mountain. It has some of the more advanced runs.

"Sure! we can hit La Balma," your dad says. "It's a 6-mile run. I heard they've gotten a lot of fresh snow there. It'll make for some great skiing."

You and your dad take a cable-car ride up the side of the mountain. Then, it's a long hike with skis strapped to your back. Finally, you find yourself more than a mile up on the mountain. There is not another skier in sight and snowy slopes fill the landscapes.

It's cold and windy, but you still take a quick break to eat a snack. This run will take you all afternoon to get down. You'll need your energy.

"Are you ready for this?" your dad asks as he slips his ski boots into the bindings.

"Yeah," you say.

You wonder how you should ski down. You could bomb downhill. It'd be exciting to see how fast you can go down a mountain you've never skied before. Or maybe you should slowly wind your way down. That way, you could maintain control of your speed.

TO GO STRAIGHT DOWN, GO TO PAGE 61.
TO WIND YOUR WAY DOWN, TURN TO PAGE 63.

You turn your skis and push off, straight down the slope. You feel the wind rush past you. You hear the swoosh of your skis cutting through the snow. Even though it's fresh snow, you quickly pick up speed. You leave your dad behind.

The mountain slope is much steeper than the ski hill you are used to back home. Soon, you are going at an uncontrollable speed as you slice through the snow. You lean to the left, trying to slow yourself down. But as you do, your skis sweep out from under you. You hit the ground hard and slide headfirst down the slope.

Your fall stops as you crash into a rocky outcropping sticking out of the snow. Luckily, you were wearing a helmet. But when you try to stand, you feel woozy.

TURN THE PAGE.

"Whoa, sit back down for a bit," your dad says when he reaches you. "You don't look so good."

Your dad helps you the rest of the way down the mountain. At the hospital, the doctor says that you have a concussion. That not only puts an end to your day of skiing, but that means you won't be skiing for the rest of the trip. You're so upset. All you can do is watch other skiers enjoying their vacation at Monterosa Ski.

THE END

TO FOLLOW ANOTHER PATH, TURN TO PAGE 11.

You are on an unfamiliar mountain on a steep slope in the middle of nowhere. You don't want to rush downhill. There could be dangers you do not know about. And the slopes here are steeper than you are used to.

You lean left, letting the edge of your skis cut into the snow. You head down the slope at an angle. Then you lean right to cut back across the slope, zigzagging your way down.

As you ski along, you shoot through gaps between rocky outcrops. You ski through open bowls of snow.

You start to feel more comfortable on the mountain. As your confidence builds, you push yourself a little more. Instead of winding back and forth in wide sweeping arcs, you start to bomb down some of the slopes a little faster. It is exciting to feel the rush of the wind.

TURN THE PAGE.

To your right, you see a steep ridge. It has a mound of fresh snow on top of it. It could be fun to race down. To your left, you see small drop offs. You could fly over them into the valley below instead.

TO GO RIGHT AND RACE DOWN THE RIDGE, GO TO PAGE 65.
TO GO LEFT AND FLY OVER THE DROP OFFS, TURN TO PAGE 68.

You lean right and shoot for the ridge. You ski along it, looking for a good spot to race down into the valley.

The wind is especially blustery here, out in the open. It has caused the snow to drift and form a shelf overhanging the ridge. You don't notice this as you are skiing along. Not until it's too late.

The shelf of snow collapses beneath your skis, and the world drops out from under you. Suddenly, you are tumbling down the mountain in an avalanche of snow.

Everything is white. Your skis are ripped from your feet. Your shoulder slams into a rock. You grasp for anything with your hands, but nothing helps you.

When you finally stop, you feel groggy. You try to move your arms to push yourself up, but they are pinned down by the snow. You try to lift your legs. You can't move!

TURN THE PAGE.

You start to panic. You scream. You try to jerk your arms free. But none of it matters. You are buried under tons of snow.

But that's not the worst of it. You have little air to breathe. Soon your consciousness starts to fade. As you black out, all you can do is hope that your dad escaped the avalanche.

THE END

TO FOLLOW ANOTHER PATH, TURN TO PAGE 11.

Seeing the snow built up atop the ridges worries you. It has recently snowed. There is always the risk of an avalanche on steep slopes with a lot of snow buildup.

Instead, you opt for the drop offs. You have gone off jumps at home. You know you can handle them.

You shoot over one of the drop offs and the world falls away. It feels as if you're falling forever until *POOF!* The snow meets your skis. It surprises you a little, how far you flew down the steep slope. But the powdery snow cushions your landing.

You look back to see your dad following you. You're surprised to see him spin through the air before landing in a puff of snow.

The rest of the day is spent winding back and forth on the mountain side. You shoot down into valleys and wind your way through an evergreen forest. At one point, you stop to take a break and look at a frozen waterfall.

By time you reach the bottom of the mountain, you are happily exhausted. You survived your first attempt at big mountain skiing.

THE END

TO FOLLOW ANOTHER PATH, TURN TO PAGE 11.

CHAPTER 4

HELI-SKIING

Skiing the remote areas of Alaska is one of the most extreme things you can imagine. You jump at the chance. This will be a trip of a lifetime and something to brag about to your friends.

"Alaska would be amazing," you say to your dad.

"Then let's do it," he replies. "It's something I've always wanted to do. Now's our chance."

That night, you video chat with your friends. You can't wait to tell them where you are going.

"That is super cool," Tou says.

"The mountains up there will dwarf our little ski hill," Tess adds.

"I'll need to get in some practice runs before we leave," you say.

The next few days, you meet up with your friends at the ski hill in town. You want to make sure you are ready for the challenging skiing in Alaska.

One night after skiing with your friends, your dad tells you two outfitters have openings in Alaska. Outfitters are companies that make many of the arrangements for your trip, such as providing gear and guidance. One opening is out of Haines, which is on Alaska's panhandle. The area has some of the tallest coastal mountains in the world. It is known for its light, dry snow. This is easy, fast snow to ski through. Plus, you can do some free-ride skiing through many ungroomed trails.

The other is in Valdez. This is where heli-skiing began. It's along the Gulf of Alaska, in the south-central part of the state.

The area receives upward of 58 feet of snow a year. It's heavy and moist. While tougher to ski through, the snow provides better support on steep slopes.

"So, where are we going?" your dad asks.

TO GO TO HAINES, TURN TO PAGE 74.
TO GO TO VALDEZ, TURN TO PAGE 78.

"Let's check out Haines," you say. You nudge your dad in the arm and add, "If it's too much for you, we can always go to a ski resort in Juneau. Maybe they have a hot tub you can rest in."

"Too much for *me*?" your dad laughs. "This is gonna be some of the most extreme skiing you've ever imagined."

Just getting to Haines is an adventure. The Alaskan Panhandle is a narrow stretch of land tucked between the Gulf of Alaska on the west and British Columbia on the east. It's a mountainous region, filled with numerous islands and fjords. To get to your final destination, you have to take a series of small planes and ferries.

And that's just the beginning. You spend a night in Haines, a town of a little more than 1,500 people that is surrounded by snow-capped mountains.

You hop into a helicopter the next morning. Inside are half a dozen people, including your ski guide and the pilot. You watch as your ski gear is loaded into a cage attached to one of the helicopter's landing skids.

The helicopter lifts off. Soon, you are zooming above the mountain. Snowy peaks fill the horizon.

"We can ski any of this," your ski guide says, motioning out the window. "And yesterday, I scoped out a perfect spot for us."

Soon, the helicopter drops you off in a white landscape. Snow stretches out as far as you can see. You aren't at the top of a mountain, but still you're high up.

"In a few hours, the helicopter will meet us down the mountain," the guide says. "I'll show you the way, but it's up to you how fast you get there."

TO SPEED DOWN THE HILL, TURN TO PAGE 81.
TO TAKE IT SLOW AND WIND YOUR WAY DOWNHILL, TURN TO PAGE 84.

"Valdez is a classic destination," you say. "After all, it's where heli-skiing became a thing."

"Then that's the plan," your dad says.

To get to Valdez, you have to catch a flight to Anchorage, Alaska's largest city. Then it's a short flight in a prop plane to your final destination. Valdez is a coastal town of more than 3,000 people, tucked into the Chugach Mountain Range. You are amazed at how the snowy peaks fill the horizon.

You and your dad rest up for a day. The next morning, it's time to head out.

"Be sure to get all of your gear ready," your dad tells you.

You grab your ski boots, goggles, and a helmet.

GO TO PAGE 80.

You look at your skis. Should you bring them with you? After all, you've used them for years. But you read somewhere that people use special skis for places like this.

TO BRING YOUR OWN SKIS, TURN TO PAGE 86.
TO USE THE SPECIAL SKIS, TURN TO PAGE 88.

You're on a mountain with the steepest slopes you've ever seen. You could really test your limits. You want to see how fast you can make it down the mountain.

You turn to your dad and shout, "Race ya!"

Then you are off downhill. You feel the wind in your face and hear the swoosh of your skis cutting through the snow.

You started off on a fairly flat spot. But the terrain quickly changes to a steep descent. On top of that, the snow is easy to ski through. You start racing down incredibly fast. The world passes you in a blur.

You start to get nervous. You try to turn and slow down. But suddenly, your skis are ripped out from under your feet. You tumble headfirst down the mountain.

TURN THE PAGE.

You are out of breath when you finally come to a stop. You sit up and stretch out your limbs to make sure you haven't broken anything. You hurt all over but nothing feels broken.

A moment later, your dad and the guide ski up next to you.

"Are you okay?" your dad asks breathlessly, bending down next to you. "You scared me."

"Yeah, I'm okay," you say, trying to smile. But even doing that hurts.

"It's a good thing you stopped before your skis did," the ski guide says. "I think they're halfway down the mountain by now."

Great, no skis, you think.

This means that instead of enjoying a day of skiing, you will be walking down the mountain.

You still have to reach the spot where the helicopter will pick you up. It will be a long and difficult hike through the snow.

THE END

TO FOLLOW ANOTHER PATH, TURN TO PAGE 11.

This isn't like the ski hill at home, where you know every turn. You've never been on a mountain like this in your life. You have no idea what to expect. You decide that it's best to just take it slow and enjoy the way down.

You head in the direction that the guide went. You lean left and feel the edge of your skis cutting into the light snow. You turn in a slow, sweeping arc. Then you lean right, kicking up a trail of snow behind you.

It's a gorgeous day. With the sun glinting off the snow, you feel like you're in a winter wonderland.

At one point, the guide cuts into a deep valley. Although it looks like a pretty steep drop, he makes it look easy. You could follow him. Or you could look for a less steep route.

TO FOLLOW THE GUIDE, TURN TO PAGE 91.
TO FIND A ROUTE THAT IS NOT AS STEEP, TURN TO PAGE 94.

You decide to pack your own skis. After all, they are the ones you are used to skiing with.

Soon, you and your dad find yourselves inside a helicopter, along with the pilot. The helicopter's blades whir loudly overhead.

"We should be at our destination in about half an hour," the pilot shouts.

That destination is a small plateau near the top of a mountain. The helicopter lands and you all get off. As the helicopter lifts off, your dad shoots down the hill. You put on the skis you brought and follow after him.

You are amazed at how easy he makes it look, skiing back and forth in wide, sweeping loops down the steep sides of the mountain.

As soon as you get off the plateau and start downhill, you struggle.

Your skis are stiff and narrow. While perfect for the ski hill back home, they sink into the untouched snow on these steep slopes. You have difficulty turning and end up tumbling downhill.

You feel like an amateur, falling over and over again. Instead of enjoying the mountain, you spend most of your time picking yourself up from the snow.

THE END

TO FOLLOW ANOTHER PATH, TURN TO PAGE 11.

Different styles of skis work better for different types of snow and terrain. Your dad asks a ski guide to help you find the right skis.

"These skis will be a bit more flexible than what you're used to," the ski guide tells you. "But that'll make it easier to turn in this heavy snow."

"They're wider than mine," you say as you pick up one of the skis.

"We're not skiing hard-packed groomed trails," she says. "Wider skis will keep you from sinking into untouched snow."

Soon, you find yourself ducking into a helicopter as its blades whir overhead. Inside, there are five other people: your dad, two other skiers, the pilot, and your ski guide.

You take off, and soon you are zooming over towering white peaks. The helicopter drops you off on a small plateau high up in the mountains.

"We'll get picked up downhill in a few hours," your guide says. "So just get your gear ready, and I'll lead the way."

You stand at the edge of the plateau looking down. It must be a 45-degree drop.

"Are you ready for this?" your dad asks.

"Yeah," you say, but you are nervous. "This is steeper than I thought it would be."

"Just follow me," your dad says reassuringly.

He begins skiing down the slope, going back and forth in long, sweeping arcs. You head down and follow him.

TURN THE PAGE.

You've been skiing for years. You know that skiing like this is fairly easy. The slope is steep. But you're skiing along the side of the mountain, not straight down. You're able to control your speed.

You sweep down slopes and glide through valleys. You're having the time of your life. You want to check in with your dad and see how he's doing. Right now, he is slowly winding his way back and forth down a steep slope. It's slow going, so you could catch up to him. Or maybe you should wait until he gets down somewhere not as steep.

TO SKI UP TO YOUR DAD ON THE SLOPE, TURN TO PAGE 95.
TO WAIT UNTIL YOUR DAD IS OFF THE SLOPE, TURN TO PAGE 98.

The guide knows his way around these mountains. He knows where the dangers are and where it is safe to ski. So even though it's a steep drop, you follow. You make big sweeping arcs down the slope to control your speed. At one point, you feel unsteady and decide to snow plow. You bring the tips of your skis together in front of you and form a V shape. It slows you down even more.

Your dad waits for you at the bottom of the slope.

"Nice job!" he shouts. "All that practice paid off."

You smile and then shoot ahead, continuing down the mountain.

It is a long, exhausting day of skiing. But you ski within your limits and follow the guide.

TURN THE PAGE.

When you finally reach the waiting helicopter, you practically collapse inside. You're tired, but feeling proud to have successfully skied this remote wilderness.

THE END

TO FOLLOW ANOTHER PATH, TURN TO PAGE 11.

Between the steep descent and the snow, you decide to play it safe. Your guide is far enough ahead that he doesn't see you follow the ridge along the edge of the valley.

The valley spreads out below you on one side of the ridge. You are surprised to see nothing on the other side. It's like you're skiing along a cliff face! What you don't realize is that the ridge is actually a shelf of snow hanging over a towering cliff. Not until it is too late!

Your weight causes the snow to collapse. Suddenly, you are in the air. There is nothing you can do. You fall hundreds of feet to the rock below. You should have followed your guide. He would have known about the ridge. Now, your broken body lies buried beneath many feet of snow.

THE END

TO FOLLOW ANOTHER PATH, TURN TO PAGE 11.

Your dad is taking his time skiing down the slope. It's the perfect moment to catch up to him. While he is sweeping back and forth across the side of the mountain, you aim downhill to catch him.

On the steep slope, it's easy to pick up speed—even in this heavy snow. You catch up with your dad before he's even halfway down. Then you lean into the hill to ski alongside him.

"Hey, Dad!" you shout.

Just as he turns to you, you feel the snow shift under your feet. On this steep section of mountain, you and your dad's weight have caused the snow to shift. It begins to slide down the mountain. Avalanche!

Suddenly, you are tumbling down the slope head over heels. Snow is everywhere, but it doesn't cushion you as you bang against rocks on the way down.

TURN THE PAGE.

When you finally stop rolling, you are chest deep in a pile of snow. You are sore, but nothing feels broken.

"Dad?" you shout, wondering where he is.

There is no sign of him. You don't know if he slid farther down the mountain or if he's buried in snow.

"Dad!" you shout again.

There is no response.

Somewhere in this fast expanse of snow, your dad is lost and you can't help him. You are stuck. You desperately start digging at the tightly packed snow. All the while, you are shouting for help. Hopefully someone will hear you soon and come to the rescue.

THE END

TO FOLLOW ANOTHER PATH, TURN TO PAGE 11.

You decide to wait for a better chance to catch up to your dad. On steep slopes like this, skiing can be difficult. The snow can be treacherous. If it gets disturbed too much, it can shift and start sliding down the mountain in an avalanche.

You sweep back and forth, slowly making your way down as your dad cuts into a valley. Shortly after that, you find him standing next to your guide on a wide ridge. They are waiting for the rest of the skiers.

You slide up to your dad.

"What do you think?" he asks.

"This is amazing," you say.

And it truly is. The rest of the day you spend winding your way down the mountain. Towering peaks rise up all around. The snowy landscape fills the horizon. The air is crisp and fresh.

You are exhausted by time you reach the waiting helicopter. But it was well worth it. You've finished your first big mountain skiing trip. It's something that you will never forget.

THE END

TO FOLLOW ANOTHER PATH, TURN TO PAGE 11.

CHAPTER 5

SKIING THROUGH HISTORY

For thousands of years, people have strapped wooden planks onto their feet and skied across the snow. During prehistoric times, hunters used skis to follow game animals as they moved across wintry landscapes.

Skiing is faster than walking. Top cross-country skiers can reach speeds of 20 miles (32 kilometers) per hour over long distances. Downhill skiers can fly down at more than 75 miles (121 km) per hour.

Skiing started to become more than just a means of getting around in the mid-1700s. The Norwegian army held competitions in which soldiers skied across snowfields and fired at targets.

Eventually this developed into the sport of biathlon. Some of the first ski races were held in Norway in the mid-1800s. These events piqued people's interest in skiing as a recreational activity.

Early skiing was called Nordic, or cross country, skiing. But the development of alpine skiing truly helped grow the sport of skiing. People enjoyed the rush of speeding down mountain slopes. By the late 1880s, the popularity of downhill skiing had spread from Europe to other parts of the world, including the United States.

In 1924, Nordic skiing events and ski jumping were part of the first Winter Olympics. It was held at the Chamonix Mont Blanc ski resort in southern France. Then in 1936, alpine skiing became part of the Winter Games. Racers took one run downhill. Then the next day, they raced a slalom run, zigzagging between markers. The skiers with the fastest times won medals.

In 1948, slalom skiing became its own event at the Winter Olympics.

In the 1930s, the tow rope and chairlift were invented. Before then, skiers had to carry their skis up the slopes they planned to ski down. These inventions made it easier to get up the hill. They also gave rise to ski resorts dedicated to skiing.

Skiing has continued to evolve over the years. In the 1950s, metal skis began to replace wooden ones. And in the 1960s, plastic ski boots replaced leather ones. Metal skis and plastic boots were more durable and of higher quality, giving skiers better control on the slopes. These changes helped make the sport less expensive and available to more people.

Some of the top skiers started looking for new challenges, such as skiing down the world's tallest mountains. This gave rise to big mountain, or extreme, skiing.

Big mountain skiers would climb and ski down some of the highest mountains in the world, such as Mount Kilimanjaro in Tanzania. This is a sport for only the most adventurous skiers.

Up until the late 1900s, most ski resorts did not allow skiers to do jumps or tricks on their runs. People thought it was dangerous and disruptive to other skiers. But with the growing popularity of snowboarding, a new feature started popping up at ski resorts in the 1980s. Terrain parks are skate parks made out of snow. They include many of the same obstacles, such as jumps to rails and halfpipes. Both snowboarders and skiers use these obstacles to perform tricks.

With the freedom to jump, flip, and perform all sorts of tricks, freestyle skiing became popular. Freestyle is a combination of skiing and acrobatics. It includes racing, flying over jumps, and doing stunts.

Freestyle skiing became an Olympic sport in 1988. It remains one of the most dramatic events at the Winter Games.

Today, there is a style of skiing for just about everyone. Cross country skiers glide through wooded trails. Downhill skiers wind their way down mountainous slopes. Freestyle skiers flip through the air doing tricks. Big mountain skiers tackle some of the world's steepest slopes. Skiing has gone from being a way to get around in snow to one of the most popular winter sports.

BRIEF BIOGRAPHIES

Big mountain skiing is one the most challenging forms of skiing. Swiss skier Sylvain Saudan is considered one of the pioneers of the sport. In the late 1960s, he began skiing down some incredibly steep slopes in the Alps. His feats earned him the title *skieur de l'impossible*, or "skier of the impossible." People did not believe certain slopes could be skied down, including Mont Blanc in the Alps. But Saudan did it.

In 1982, Saudan made the *Guinness World Records* for his daring skiing. He conquered Gasherbrun I in the Himalayas. He became the first person to ski down a mountain taller than 26,000 feet (8,000 meters).

Japanese skier Yuichiro Miura also showed what extreme feats could be done on skis. In 1966, he skied down Japan's tallest peak, Mount Fuji. That same year, he also tackled Denali, the tallest mountain in North America. In 1967, Miura attempted to ski down Mount Everest, the tallest peak in the world. But Miura crashed after 4,200 feet (1,281 m). That did not stop Miura from conquering Mount Kilimanjaro, the tallest mountain in Africa. Miura also became the first person to ski down Mount Vinson, the highest peak in Antarctica.

Doug Coombs won the first big mountain extreme skiing contest in Alaska and helped bring extreme skiing to the United States. Coombs tackled some of the world's tallest peaks, from Mount Vinson in Antarctica to Wyatt Peak in Kyrgyzstan. He even helped establish heli-skiing in Alaska.

More recently, skiers such as Ingrid Backstrom are defining the sport of big mountain skiing. Backstrom has skied some of the towering peaks on Greenland and on Baffin Island, Canada's largest island. She has also tackled Reddomaine, a 20,000-foot (6,096-m) peak in China. With her aggressive style on the slopes, Backstrom has won several freeskiing competitions and has been featured in more than 20 films on skiing.

K2 in Pakistan is the second tallest mountain in the world. Many consider it the most difficult to climb. In 2018, Polish skier Andrzej Bargiel became the first person to survive skiing down its treacherous slopes. It took Bargiel just over 8 hours to make it down the 28,251 foot (8,611 m) mountain.

OTHER PATHS TO EXPLORE

1. In the Whistler Blackcomb story path, you hit the halfpipe with your snowboard. Imagine you are skiing the halfpipe. What tricks would you try?

2. In heli-skiing, skiers are dropped off in unfamiliar, dangerous areas with no groomed trails. What kinds of dangers would these skiers face?

3. People have tried to ski parts of Mount Everest, the tallest peak in the world. Others have tried skiing down K2, the second tallest mountain in the world. Imagine you are an extreme skier. Which mountain would you choose and why? How would you plan for your trip?

GLOSSARY

alpine (AL-pyn)—downhill skiing

avalanche (AH-vuh-lanch)—a large mass of ice, snow, or earth that suddenly moves down a mountain

backcountry (BAK-kuhn-tree)—an isolated area often at high altitude that is not marked by trails

biathlon (BYE-ah-thuh-lohn)—a winter sports event that combines cross-country skiing and rifle sharpshooting

cable car (KAY-buhl KAHR)—a large aerial lift that transports skiers and snowboarders up the slopes

concussion (kuhn-KUH-shuhn)—an injury to the brain caused by a hard blow to the head

dislocate (DIS-loh-kayt)—to separate a bone from the joint

fjord (fee-ORD)—a narrow inlet of ocean between high cliffs

gondola (GON-duh-luh)—an enclosed, aerial lift that is faster than an open chairlift

halfpipe (HAF-pipe)—a U-shaped ramp with high walls

perpendicular (PUR-pend-ik-yoo-luhr)—straight up and down relative to another surface

powder (POW-duhr)—fresh snow that hasn't been packed down

prehistoric (pree-hi-STOR-ik)—from a time before history was recorded

rail (RAYL)—a metal bar found on snow parks built for freestyle skiers and snowboarders

run (RUHN)—one ride from the start of the course to the finish

READ MORE

Carr, Aaron. *Skiing.* New York: AV2, 2020.

Smith, Elliot. *Freeskiing and Other Extreme Snow Sports.* North Mankato, MN: Capstone Press, 2020.

Tomljanovic, Tatiana. *Skiing.* New York: AV2 by Weigl, 2021.

INTERNET SITES

Freestyle skiing
https://usskiandsnowboard.org/teams/freestyle

Whistler Blackcomb terrain park
https://www.whistlerblackcomb.com/the-mountain/about-the-mountain/terrain-parks.aspx

INDEX

Alagna Valsesia, 58
Alaska, 9, 11, 71, 72, 74, 78
    Haines, 72, 74
    Valdez, 72, 78
avalanches, 65, 66, 68, 95, 98

backcountry skiing, 10, 49, 52, 56
biathlons, 102
Blackcomb Peak, 13, 20
British Columbia, 9, 10, 74

freeskiing, 10

gondolas, 13
    New Blackcomb Gondola, 20
    Whistler Village Gondola, 29,
      31

halfpipes, 13, 20, 22, 24, 25, 26, 28,
    33, 37, 39, 42, 44, 45, 46, 104
    Superpipe, 22
helicopters, 11, 76, 83, 86, 88, 89,
    92, 99
heli-skiing, 11, 72, 78

Italy, 9, 10, 49, 51, 52

La Balma, 58

Mont Blanc, 54
Monte Rosa, 10
Monterosa Ski, 10, 49, 50, 51, 52,
    58, 62

Norwegian army, 101

terrain parks, 10, 13, 14, 22, 29, 31,
    42, 104
tricks, 10, 13, 14, 19, 22, 25, 26, 28,
    29, 30, 31, 32, 33, 36, 37, 39, 40,
    42, 44, 45, 104, 105
    180s, 36, 40
    270s, 41
    360s, 24, 31
    air-to-fakies, 26
    butter, 28
    frontside 360s, 28
    frontside 540s, 24, 26, 37, 44

Whistler Blackcomb, 13, 14, 15, 19
Whistler Mountain, 13, 29, 31
Winter Olympics, 10, 102, 103